ABC I Love Me

Miriam Muhammad

ABC I Love Me

ISBN: 978-0-692-14977-5

Published by Choose Joy Publishing

For my son, Maaz, and every little black & brown boy and girl. You are more than enough. Choose joy!

A is for Afro
My curly afro is amazing!

B is for Beautiful
I am beautiful !

C is for Confident
I am confident !

D is for Divine
I am a divine creation. A part of God!

E is for Enthusiastic
I am excited about life!

F is for Fearless
I am fearless!

G is for Gratitude
I am grateful for everything in my life!

H is for Healthy
I am in perfect health!

I is for Imagination
I use my imagination to create greatness!

J is for Joy
I choose joy!

K is for King
My father is a King!

L is for Love
I love myself!

M is for Magical
I am magical!

N is for Notable
I am notable!

O is for Original
I am Original !

P is for Positive
I am positive !

Q is for Queen
My mother is a queen !

R is for Royalty
I am royalty !

S is for Skin
I adore my brown skin !

T is for Talented
I have many talents!

V is for Victory
I am a champion. I will win !

W is for Worthy
I am worthy of the best !

X is for X- ray
My body was created
especially for me !

Y is for Yes
I like to try new things !

Z is for Zoom
I can run very fast !

ACKNOWLEDGEMENTS

I would like to thank The Divine Creator for my gifts and talents. Thank you to my amazing husband, Akeem, for his constant support and encouragement. Thank you to my son, Maaz, for being my motivation for sharing this project with the world. Thank you to my parents (Sharrieff and Sharrieffah), my siblings (Joshua, Naeemah, and Rashad), and my brother-in-law (Jamal) for the constant inspiration and enthusiasm you showed about this book. Thank you to my forever friends, my girls, for always being in my corner. A huge thank you to my friend and Soror (Kendra) for being an excellent advisor, consultant, and guiding light on this literary journey. Thanks to the late Marion Ball, my grandmother, who always believed in me and taught me to believe in myself. Thank you to each and every parent and child who purchased this book. May you always be the light you seek.